TOURIST TR...

Written by Cas Lester

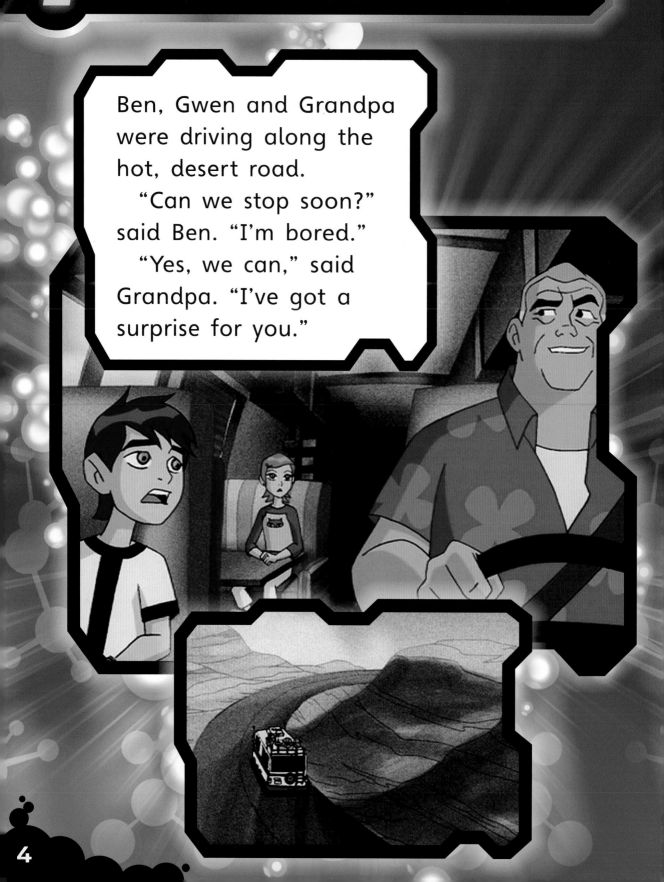

Ben, Gwen and Grandpa were driving along the hot, desert road.

"Can we stop soon?" said Ben. "I'm bored."

"Yes, we can," said Grandpa. "I've got a surprise for you."

Soon, they pulled up in a dusty street.

"Welcome to Sparksville!" said Grandpa.

"Sparksville? More like Dullsville!" said Ben.

Grandpa gave them tickets to see something called 'IT'.

Ben and Gwen went into a
big, dark room. Inside was a
huge ball made of rubber bands.
"Is this IT?" asked Gwen.
"What a joke!"

Ben wanted to have some fun and decided to use the Omnitrix. "I know," he said. "Four Arms!"

Ben turned into Four Arms and started throwing the ball around. "Don't miss the big ball game," he laughed.

"Careful Ben," said Gwen. "Look out!"

CRASH!

THUMP! Four Arms dropped the ball and it crashed out of the building. He couldn't stop it!

At last, the huge ball stopped in the middle of the main street.

"No problem," said Four Arms to Gwen. "I'll just put it back."

But at that moment, Four Arms turned back into Ben. Now he couldn't lift the ball!

"Now what are we going to do?" asked Gwen.
"Don't worry," said Ben. "It will all be OK."

But it wasn't OK. The next morning, they could see that the town had been smashed to pieces. There was smoke everywhere and strange electric sparks were jumping around. What had happened?

The Mayor told them that the rubber band ball had once been used to trap an alien. When Four Arms dropped the ball the day before, the alien had escaped.

It was an electrical alien called a Megawhatt, and now it was making trouble!

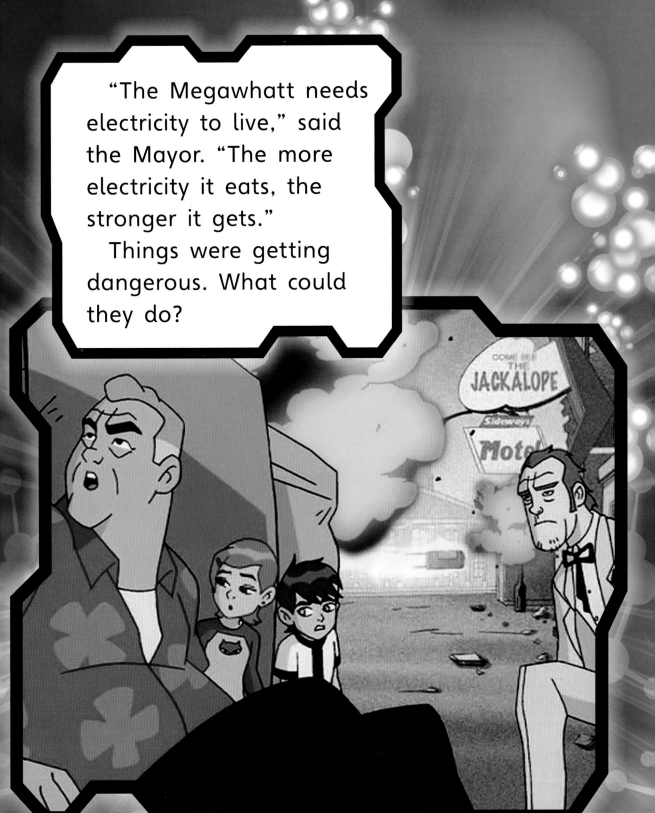

"The Megawhatt needs electricity to live," said the Mayor. "The more electricity it eats, the stronger it gets."

Things were getting dangerous. What could they do?

Ben had a plan. He turned into Upgrade and tried to catch the Megawhatt, but it was too fast.
   After a few minutes, Upgrade turned back into Ben. What could he do now?

Then Gwen had an idea. What if they could trap the alien under the ground? They found a big electric sign and pushed one end into the ground. The Megawhatt followed it and was gone!

Everyone thought that the Megawhatt was gone for good. But then hundreds of Megawhatts appeared. The first Megawhatt had eaten some electric cables. Now it had multiplied!

There was a BANG! Then a huge THUD! The Megawhatts had taken over a planet display from the space museum. They were walking out of town!

"The Megawhatts are going to the power station," said Gwen. "They want more electricity!" Ben acted fast. He used the Omnitrix to turn into Heatblast.

Then Gwen had another idea. "Quick, Grandpa, let's get that giant fishbowl from the top of the aquarium!"

Gwen told Heatblast to follow the Megawhatts to the power station.

At the power station, Heatblast threw firebolts at the Megawhatts. But the Megawhatts ate them up and came back for more.

Gwen and Grandpa fetched the fishbowl. They took it back to the power station and covered it with a giant cloth.

"Heatblast! Over here!" shouted Gwen.

Heatblast flew to the fishbowl. The Megawhatts wanted more electricity, so they followed him.

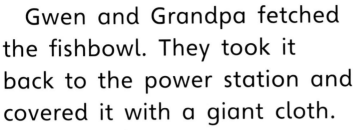

At the last moment, Heatblast pulled at the cloth and jumped out of the way. The Megawhatts couldn't stop and they flew into the fishbowl. SLAM! A lid came down and they were trapped.

"Using the fishbowl to trap the Megawhatts was a great idea," said Grandpa. "They aren't going anywhere now!"

Just then, Heatblast turned back
into Ben. "I think these guys need
to cool off!" he said. "I guess
there's only one bright spark in
town now," he added.

"Yes, and that's *so* not you!"
said Gwen!